My Grandpa Died Today

illustrated by Stewart Kranz

 **HUMAN SCIENCES PRESS, INC.**
72 FIFTH AVENUE
NEW YORK, N.Y. 10011

In memory of Grandpa Max

My grandpa was very, very old. He was much, much older than me. He was much older than my mother and father. He was much older than all my aunts and uncles. He was even a little bit older than the white haired bakery-man down the block.

My grandpa taught me how to play checkers. And he read stories to me. And he helped me build my first model. And he showed me how to reach out with my bat and hit a curve ball. And he always rooted for my team.

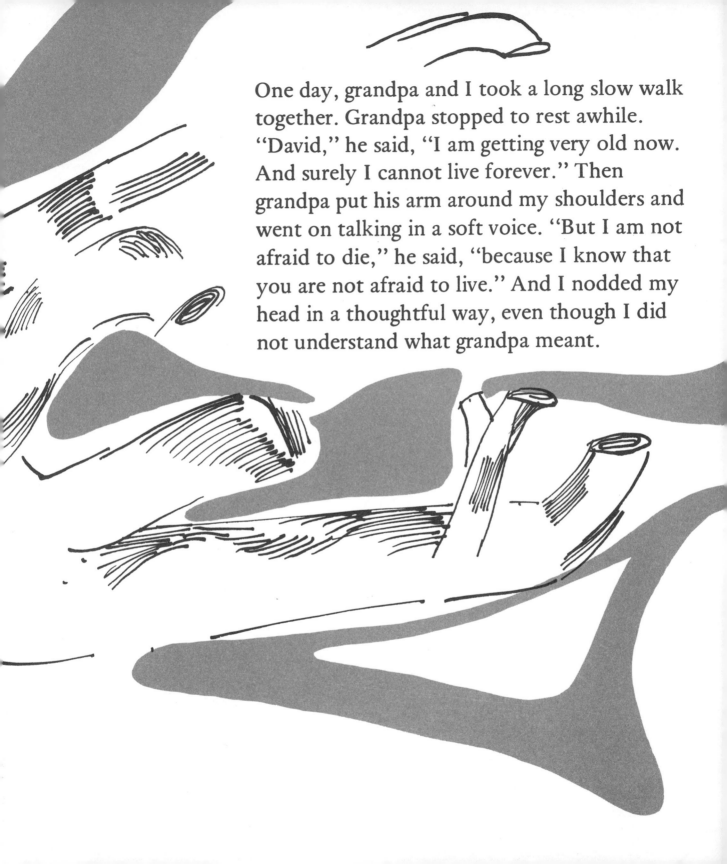

One day, grandpa and I took a long slow walk together. Grandpa stopped to rest awhile. "David," he said, "I am getting very old now. And surely I cannot live forever." Then grandpa put his arm around my shoulders and went on talking in a soft voice. "But I am not afraid to die," he said, "because I know that you are not afraid to live." And I nodded my head in a thoughtful way, even though I did not understand what grandpa meant.

Just two days later grandpa sat down in our
big white rocking chair. And he rocked
himself for a little while. Then, very softly,
very quietly, grandpa closed his eyes.

And he stopped rocking.
And he didn't move any more.
And he didn't talk any more.
And he didn't breathe any more.
And the grownups said that grandpa died.

My mother cried and cried. And my father cried and cried. And many people came to our house. And they cried, too. And they took grandpa away and buried him.

More people kept coming to our house. And
they pulled down all the window shades. And
they covered all the mirrors. And our whole
house looked as if it was going to cry. Even
the red shingles on the roof. Even the white
shutters at the windows. Even the flagstone
steps going up to the door. And everyone was
very sad.

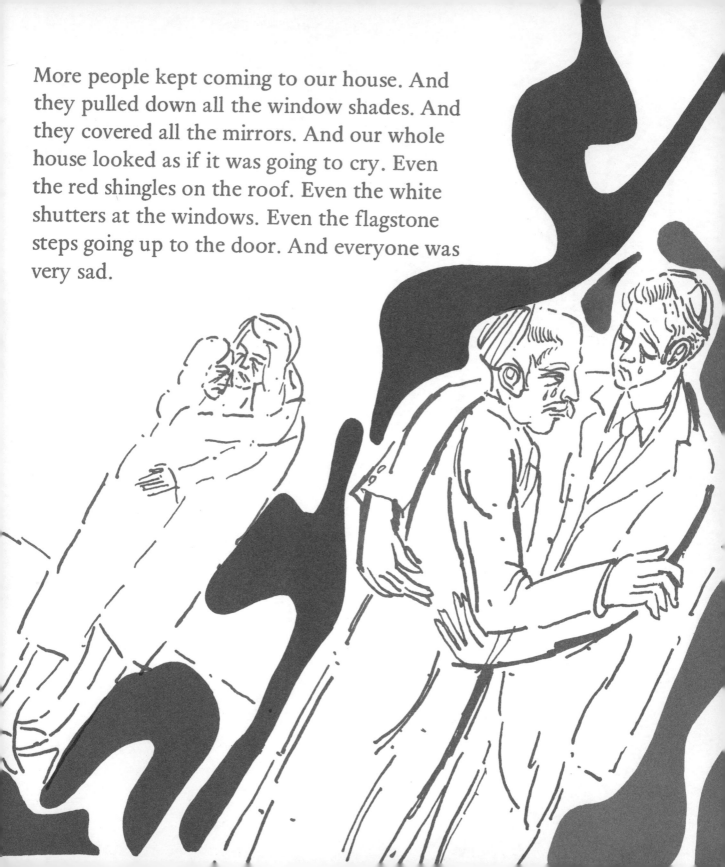

I was sad, too. I thought about my grandpa
and about all the things we used to do
together. And, in a little while, I discovered a
funny, empty, scary, rumbly kind of feeling
at the bottom of my stomach. And some tears
streaming down my cheeks.

Somehow, I didn't feel like sitting in the
living room with all the gloomy grown-ups. So
I walked quietly into my own room, and I
took out some of my favorite toys. Then I did
two jig-saw puzzles and colored three
pictures. And I rolled a few marbles very
slowly across the floor.

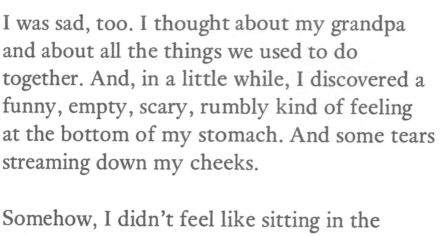

The grownups didn't mind at all. They came in and smiled at me. And someone patted me gently on my head. It was almost as if they all knew that grandpa and I must have had some very special talks together.

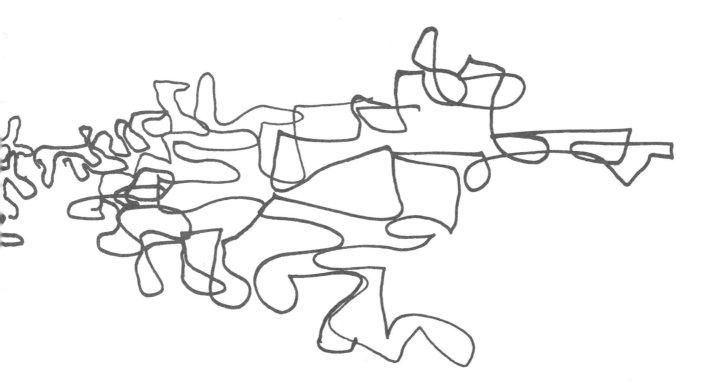

The next day was still a very sad day at our house. Late in the afternoon, I heard a soft knock at the door. My best friend, Bobby, wanted to know if I could play ball. And again the grownups didn't seem to mind. So I left our sad, sorry house. And Bobby and I walked slowly down to the park.

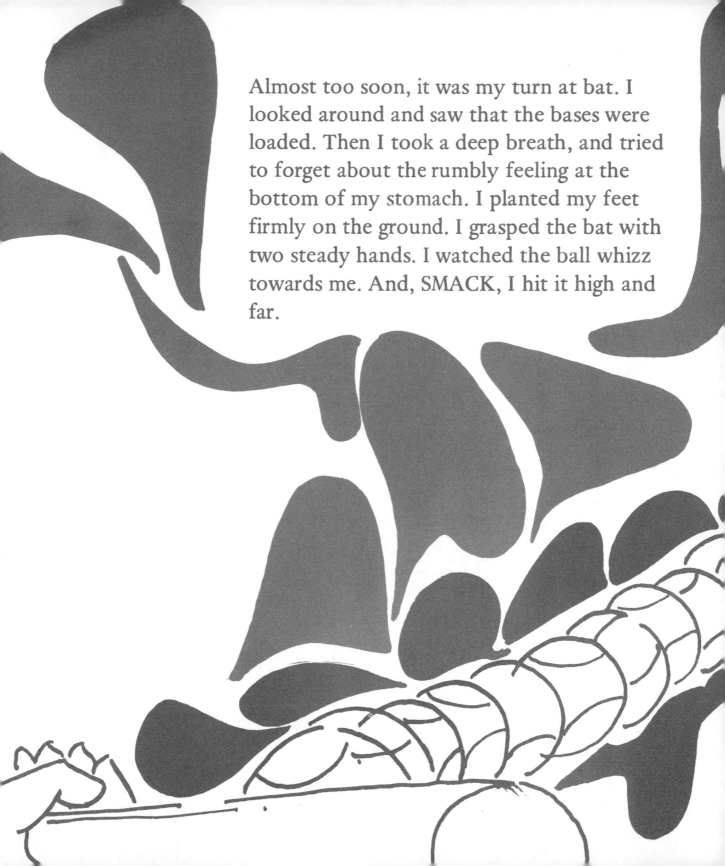

Almost too soon, it was my turn at bat. I looked around and saw that the bases were loaded. Then I took a deep breath, and tried to forget about the rumbly feeling at the bottom of my stomach. I planted my feet firmly on the ground. I grasped the bat with two steady hands. I watched the ball whizz towards me. And, SMACK, I hit it high and far.

And then I ran. I ran with every bit of strength and power and speed inside my whole body.

And it was a grand slam home run!

And somehow, right there on the field, in the middle of all the cheers and shouts of joy, I could *almost* see my grandpa's face breaking into a happy smile. And that made me feel so good inside that the rumbles in my stomach disappeared.

And the solid hardness of the ground under my feet made me feel good inside, too. And the warm touch of the sun on my cheeks made me feel good inside, too.
And, it was at that very moment, that I first began to understand why my grandpa was not afraid to die. It was because he knew that there would be many more hits and many more home runs for me. It was because he knew that I would go right on playing, and reading, and running, and laughing, and growing up.

Without really knowing why, I took off my cap. I stood very still. I looked far, far away into the clear blue sky. And I thought to myself, "Grandpa must feel good inside, too."

Then I heard the umpire calling, "Batter-up!"
And we went on with the game.

Selected Children's Books

Barbara Shook Hazen
VERY SHY
Illustrated by Shirley Chan

Barbara Shook Hazen
**IT'S A SHAME
ABOUT THE RAIN**
The Bright Side of
Disappointment
Illustrated by Bernadette Simmons

Susan Kempler ; Doreen Rappaport; and
Michele Spirn
A MAN CAN BE...
Photographs by Russell Dian

Doreen Rappaport
**"BUT SHE'S STILL MY
GRANDMA!"**
Illustrated by Bernadette Simmons

Alfred T. Stefanik , M.A.
COPYCAT SAM
Developing Ties with a Special
Child
Illustrated by Laura Huff

Barbara Jean Menzel
WOULD YOU RATHER?
Illustrated by Sumishta Brahm

Althea J. Horner , Ph.D.
LITTLE BIG GIRL
Illustrated by Patricia Rosamilia

Jo Beaudry and Lynne Ketchum
CARLA GOES TO COURT
Illustrated with Photographs by
Jack Hamilton

Linda Berman, M.A.
**THE GOODBYE
PAINTING**
Illustrated by Mark Hannon

Corinne Bergstrom
**LOSING YOUR BEST
FRIEND**
Illustrated by Patricia Rosamilia

Cilla Sheehan , M.A.C.P.
**THE COLORS THAT
I AM**
Illustrated by Glen Elliott

Polly Greenberg
**I KNOW I'M MYSELF
BECAUSE...**
Illustrated by Jennifer Barrett

Complete Children's Catalog available upon request

HUMAN SCIENCES PRESS, INC.
72 FIFTH AVENUE
NEW YORK, N.Y. 10011